Charles Dickens'

GREAT EXPECTATIONS

A retelling by
TANYA LANDMAN

Barrington Stoke

Published by Barrington Stoke
An imprint of HarperCollins*Publishers*
Westerhill Road, Bishopbriggs, Glasgow, G64 2QT

www.barringtonstoke.co.uk

HarperCollins*Publishers*
Macken House, 39/40 Mayor Street Upper,
Dublin 1, DO1 C9W8, Ireland

First published in 2024

ISBN 978-1-80090-175-9

10 9 8 7 6 5 4 3 2 1

Printed and Bound in the UK using 100% Renewable Electricity
at Martins the Printers Ltd

For Ailsa.
With thanks for everything.

My story is a long one. There are many twists and turns in my tale. Many people. Many events. All of these will slot together in the end like the pieces of a jigsaw puzzle.

But time is short.

I will be brief.

In this slim volume, I will focus on five people.

Two men. One honest; one a criminal.

Two women. One heartbroken; one who had no heart to break.

And myself: Philip Pirrip, known as Pip, who loved them all.

THE FIRST STAGE OF PIP'S GREAT EXPECTATIONS

1

My story begins on a bleak, cold Christmas Eve.

Picture this: it's late afternoon. A flat area of marshland lies beside the great grey river Thames. A chill wind is blowing across it from the distant sea. A church stands all alone in that vast wilderness. And in the graveyard, also standing all alone, is a small boy. He is reading the headstones of his mother, father and five little brothers.

The boy starts to cry.

And then a terrible shout rips the air: "Stop your noise or I'll cut your throat!"

A man rises from the ground. He is soaked to the skin, his grey clothes covered in mud. His flesh is torn and bleeding. Iron chains bind his legs.

The man grabs the boy, turns him upside down and shakes the child until his pockets have emptied. One small chunk of bread falls out, which the man eats as if he is starving.

He asks, "Where's your mother, boy?"

The boy points to the gravestone.

"Dead, eh?" the man says. "And your father too? Who do you live with?"

"My sister, sir – Mrs Joe," the boy replies. "She's the wife of Joe Gargery, the blacksmith, sir."

"Blacksmith, eh?"

The man looks at his chains.

He tells the boy to bring him food and an iron file from the blacksmith's forge first thing in the morning. He says there's a second man out on the marshes, who will eat the little boy alive if he fails to return with the goods. Then he disappears into the dark, and the terrified boy runs home.

2

That small, terrified boy was me.

I ran all the way home that Christmas Eve, but more terror lay in wait.

As I burst through the door, Joe warned me that my sister was on the rampage. She had gone out looking for me. When she returned, I was beaten with "Tickler" – the stick my sister saved for such occasions.

Joe was as strong as Hercules, but he would never stand up to my sister when she was in a rage. I later learned that Joe's father had been a violent man. Joe had seen the damage a strong man could do to his wife, and Joe was a dear, gentle soul. He had no wish to follow in his father's footsteps. Joe did his best to shield me from my sister, but both of us endured her tantrums, and it gave us a kind of bond. Joe and I were the best of friends.

And now I had to steal an iron file from him. The thought felt like a gravestone weighing me down.

*

That same night we heard the great guns firing in the marshes.

"That's another convict off," said Joe. "There was one last night too."

I asked what he meant, but my sister answered.

"They've escaped," she said. "From the hulks. The prison ships."

"Who's put into prison ships? And why?" I asked.

"People who murder," my sister said. "People who rob and do all sorts of bad things. And they always begin by asking too many questions. Get along to bed!"

I was never allowed a candle. I climbed the stairs in the dark and spent the night in terror. When I slept, I dreamt that I was drifting downriver, passing the gibbet where they hanged robbers like myself.

As soon as the black sky began to lighten, I crept down the stairs. Every floorboard seemed to scream "Stop, thief!"

I stole bread from the pantry. Cheese. Brandy. A large pork pie.

I stole a file from Joe's tools in the forge.

Then I ran for the marshes.

3

On Christmas morning, there wasn't a breath of festive cheer on the bleak, cold marsh.

A thick mist was rising. Cows and sheep suddenly appeared from it, and their mooing and baaing sounded like they were calling "Stop, thief!"

I was worn out with guilt and terror when I found the grey-clothed man. He was hunched over, his back to me, nodding, heavy with sleep. I touched him on the arm, and he turned. It was the wrong man!

I fled.

Some time later, I found the right man and delivered my stolen goods. He ate, cramming bread, cheese and pork pie into his mouth all at the same time. His eyes darted from side to side, his head cocked, listening. He had the look of a hunted animal.

He seemed lonely. Afraid. Just like me. But at least I had Joe. This man was all alone.

I said, "I'm glad you like the food."

He looked surprised. "Thankee, my boy. I do."

"Won't you leave any for him?" I asked, thinking of the second man.

"Who's him?" the man asked.

"The other one. He looked hungry."

He seemed puzzled for a moment. Then he demanded to know what the man looked like and where I had seen him. Suddenly, his look changed from the hunted to the hunter.

He crammed what food was left into his jacket pocket, then started working at the chains with Joe's file, intent on his task. I slipped away. Soon, he was gone from sight, but the sound of rasping metal rang in my ears all the way home.

4

That Christmas Day we sat down to a splendid dinner.

My sister had invited many guests, and she behaved differently whenever we had company. She was simpering and sweet, fussing over her guests while Joe and I sat silent, forbidden to speak.

I would not have minded if the guests had left me alone. But for the length of that meal, I was attacked from all sides for being ungrateful, for being bad-natured and a terrible trouble to my saintly sister. As everyone ate, my sister recited all the illnesses I had been guilty of and all the sleepless nights I had given her in my short life. She told them all the high places I had tumbled from and all the low places I had tumbled into and all the injuries I had done to myself. She listed all the times she had wished me in my grave and I had refused to go there.

Joe attempted to comfort me by pouring ever more gravy onto my plate.

I sat in terror during that Christmas dinner, waiting for the moment my sister would discover the missing pork pie. My fear rose and rose, and when she got up to fetch the pie from the pantry, I could bear it no more. I ran.

I got no further than the door.

When I pulled it open, a soldier was standing there, holding a pair of handcuffs out towards me.

5

It was not just one soldier but a whole troop of them!

It was a while before I realised they had not come for me.

The soldiers were hunting for two escaped convicts. The handcuffs they carried were broken, so they had come to the blacksmith to get them repaired.

Joe fired up the forge. When the work was done, he asked if he and I could go along with the soldiers to watch the manhunt.

What a hunt it was across the wilderness of the marsh! I rode on Joe's back while he charged at the ditches like a horse. I was so afraid that my convict would think I had betrayed him! I prayed and prayed that we would not catch him, and for a long time, my prayers were answered.

It was almost dark. Joe was almost ready to turn for home. I was sighing with relief when we heard a distant shout.

Joe was off again, running down banks, splashing into dykes, leaping over gates. The soldiers around us ran like deer.

And then everyone stopped. For there they were. Two men in the bottom of a ditch. My convict trying to kill the other one.

With water splashing and mud flying, both were dragged out by the soldiers, bleeding and panting. Yet my convict's eyes lit up with victory.

"I caught him for you!" my convict told the soldiers. "I could have escaped. But let him go free? Never!"

No one asked who the second convict was or why my convict had pursued him. The soldiers were not interested in prisoners' fights. They had to return both men to the prison ship, and it was getting dark.

The soldiers were lighting flaming torches when my convict saw me. I shook my head, desperate for him to know that I hadn't betrayed him.

He must have understood, because he said to the soldiers, "I wish to say something. It may prevent someone innocent being wrongly accused.

15

I took food from the blacksmith's." He looked at Joe. "I'm sorry to say I've eaten your pie."

"You're welcome to it," said Joe. "We don't know what you've done, but we wouldn't have you starve to death for it, would we, Pip?"

The convicts were put in a boat and rowed out to the vast prison ship. We watched them being taken up over the side. The soldiers flung their flaming torches into the water. Hissing, they went out.

My convict was gone. It was all over for him.

Joe and I turned for home.

6

I no longer feared being accused of stealing from my sister's pantry. I didn't feel guilty about giving the pie to a starving man. But I loved Joe, and when I saw him searching for his missing file, I was consumed with guilt. Yet I said nothing.

If I confessed, Joe would think me a thief. The thought of him looking at me with distrust and disappointment in his eyes was too much to bear. I was too much of a coward to do what I knew to be right. That knowledge weighed on me long after the manhunt and the convicts were forgotten.

*

A year passed. Life carried on much the same until the evening my sister returned from the market. Storming into the house, she pointed at me and declared, "If that boy ain't grateful this night, he never will be!"

I arranged my face into something that looked like gratitude but had no idea what I was to be grateful for. It was some time before my sister mentioned Miss Havisham.

I had heard of Miss Havisham. Everyone had heard of Miss Havisham.

Miss Havisham was a very rich and very peculiar old lady. She lived like a hermit in a large, gloomy house that was boarded up against the world.

My sister made the strangest announcement. Miss Havisham wanted me to go to her house and play. Even stranger was the fact my sister was utterly delighted. She was convinced that Miss Havisham might "do something" for me. But what that "something" might be, she didn't explain.

I was scrubbed to within an inch of my life and dressed up in my tightest suit. And I was delivered to Miss Havisham the following morning.

7

Satis House was the name of Miss Havisham's home. It had walled-up windows. Closed shutters. Barred doors. I stood outside the locked gates looking at the crumbling building. And then I rang the bell.

Eventually, a girl came with keys to let me in. She was painfully pretty and graceful, about my own age but so sure of herself she seemed much older. She called me "boy" and was as scornful as a queen. I fell instantly under her spell.

The girl was called Estella, and she was well named.

Estella was Latin for "star". She was exactly that.

Estella glittered. She fascinated. She was so far above me that I could only look up and marvel at her.

Some people believe our future is determined by the stars. Estella certainly determined mine.

I followed her into the dark house, along dark passages and up dark stairs. The only light came from the candle she carried. At last, we stopped outside a door.

"Go in, boy," Estella said, and walked away so I was plunged into darkness.

I did what I had been told. Opening the door, I went into a large room lit only with candles. The windows were all covered over so no sunlight could get in.

Sitting by a dressing table was the strangest lady I had ever seen.

Miss Havisham.

She wore a bridal gown. But it seemed she had not finished getting ready. One shoe was on her foot; the other lay on the table. Her bridal veil was only half arranged. And the lace and satin that should have been dazzling white was faded and yellow.

I realised that her bridal gown had been put on when she was a tall young lady. It had never been taken off and now hung loose on a body that had shrunk with age.

Miss Havisham called me to her. And when I drew near, I saw that her watch had stopped dead, the hands pointing at twenty to nine. The clock on her dressing table had stopped at the same time.

"Are you afraid?" she asked.

"No," I lied.

She put both hands to the left side of her chest and asked, "What do I touch?"

"Your heart," I said.

"Broken!" she exclaimed with an odd smile. And then she said, "Play."

Play? She could hardly have ordered anything more impossible!

"I have sick fancies," she went on. "And I want to see some play. Play! Play!"

I stood helpless, looking at her.

She told me to call Estella, so I went into the dark corridor and yelled her name.

Eventually, Estella came and the pair of us played at cards. Estella won every game. That might not have troubled me, but she was so pretty and so proud and took such pleasure in mocking me that I hardly knew what to do. Estella called me common. Stupid. Ignorant. I felt ashamed of my own existence, but Miss Havisham looked on, smiling.

At long, long last, Miss Havisham tired of watching us. Estella led me back to the courtyard and brought food for me, setting it down on the cobbles as if I were a dog.

I was left alone to eat.

When Estella came back to let me out, she saw I had been crying, and she laughed.

8

When I returned home, my sister wanted to know every detail of my strange visit. But I felt as if I'd be betraying Miss Havisham if I described her and the way she lived to my sister. Instead, I told her a ridiculous tale of Miss Havisham sitting in a velvet coach with four huge dogs. I said Miss Havisham had eaten cake from golden plates while Estella and I played with flags and swords.

My sister believed it all and muttered again that Miss Havisham surely planned to "do something" for me. Later, when my sister was washing up, I slipped into the forge to see Joe. I told him the truth: that I had been miserable at Satis House and that Estella had mocked me.

Joe was sweet and kind and good and honest. He comforted me, and I should have been grateful. But when I went to bed that night, I was haunted by the knowledge that Joe could barely read or write.

Estella would think Joe even more common and stupid and ignorant than me.

9

My second visit to Miss Havisham's was even stranger than the first. Four odd things occurred that I could make no sense of at the time.

The first was that Estella began my visit by slapping me across the face and ended it by inviting me to kiss her.

The second was that Miss Havisham placed her hand on my arm for support and made me walk with her round and round her dining room. A great wedding feast had once been laid upon the table. A feast that hadn't been eaten nor cleared away but had slowly decayed and was now covered in spiders' webs.

The third thing that startled me was the people who were there. I had thought Miss Havisham a hermit, but that day she had visitors. The first was a gentleman I met on the stairs who smelt of expensive soap. He grasped me by the throat and told me to behave.

The other guests were Miss Havisham's greedy relatives who hoped to inherit her fortune when she died. I learned they had come – as they did every year – on Miss Havisham's birthday. They all stood staring at the ruined feast, talking about someone called Matthew Pocket, who had not been to Satis House for many years. Miss Havisham said he would come only when she was dead and laid out in her coffin on the table for them all to feast upon.

After Miss Havisham's relatives had left, Estella and I played cards again, and once more I was beaten. Later, I was taken down into the yard to be fed when Miss Havisham had tired of my company.

And that is when the fourth odd thing happened.

Once I'd finished eating, Estella did not come with the keys to let me out, so I wandered into the garden. There I came across a pale young gentleman who accused me of prowling about the place and insisted on fighting me.

He did not know how to fight. He ducked and dived yet did not land a single punch. I blackened his eye and gave him a bloody nose, after which he conceded I had won and seemed perfectly cheerful about it.

When I returned to the courtyard, Estella was waiting. There was a bright flush to her face as if something had delighted her. That was when she said I could kiss her. A peck on the cheek. She offered it as if she was a queen throwing a coin to a beggar.

10

It is remarkable what a child can get used to. Very soon, I was being summoned to Miss Havisham's every other day. We must have walked miles round and round that dining table, her hand resting on my arm. When she tired of walking, I pushed her round it in a wheeled chair for hours at a stretch.

As we grew more used to each other, Miss Havisham asked me questions. What had I learned? she asked. What was I going to be? I told her I was to be apprenticed to Joe. I also told her that I knew nothing but wanted to know everything – that I was desperate for a proper education. I hoped she might help me to achieve it. But she did not. She seemed to prefer me being ignorant.

Estella was always there but never told me I might kiss her again. She was always changeable – sometimes cold, sometimes friendly, sometimes hating the very sight of me. She had so many moods, I was in a state of permanent confusion. But oh! How I adored her!

Each time I visited, Miss Havisham would ask, "Does she grow prettier and prettier, Pip?" She draped Estella with jewels and asked that same question again and again. Each time I said yes, a strange, greedy look would come over Miss Havisham's face. When we played cards, she watched Estella with the delight of a miser counting his gold. Sometimes she would embrace Estella with lavish fondness and whisper in her ear, "Break their hearts, my pride and hope. Break their hearts and have no mercy!"

It is no wonder that my thoughts were as dazed as my eyes each time I emerged from the dark of Satis House into the bright daylight.

*

My visits went on for months.

And then one awful day, Miss Havisham was walking with her hand on my arm when she said accusingly, "You are growing tall, Pip!"

That was the end of everything. Miss Havisham said it was time for me to be apprenticed. The next time I came, I was to bring Joe along with me.

11

Joe wore his Sunday best, with his shirt collar pulled up so high it made the hair on his head stand up like a tuft of feathers. He looked ridiculous, and he behaved in a ridiculous manner. As Miss Havisham interviewed us, Joe insisted on talking to me instead of her. It was as if she simply wasn't there. Estella stood by Miss Havisham's chair, her eyes laughing at the pair of us.

Miss Havisham asked if we had brought the contract for my apprenticeship. Because Joe wouldn't even look at her, I had to take the papers from his hand and give them to her. Miss Havisham gave me twenty-five guineas in payment for the work I had done at Satis House. It was to be passed on to my master, Joe Gargery, so that he could train me up to work alongside him.

Miss Havisham said goodbye and told Estella to let us out.

"Am I to come again, Miss Havisham?" I asked.

"No. Gargery is your master now."

As we were leaving, Miss Havisham suddenly called out to Joe. She said very slowly and clearly as if to a very small child, "The money is the boy's full reward. There will be no more."

The next moment, we were on the street and Estella had locked the gates against us. It was all over for me. I was cast out from Satis House. An exile. I felt like I had been tried and found guilty of the crime of being common and was now condemned to be a blacksmith.

I had liked Joe's trade. Once upon a time, I had believed the forge would be my path to manhood and independence, but that was before Estella. That simple path was spoiled for me now. I was ashamed of my home and my family.

12

Every working day, I dreaded that I would look up and see Estella peering in the windows of the forge. I knew that if she could see my blackened, grimy, common face she would laugh and laugh and laugh. And yet I missed her. I burned and ached and yearned for her. Estella, my guiding star, haunted me.

Time passed. One morning, I said very casually to Joe, "Shouldn't I pay Miss Estel— Havisham a visit?"

Joe looked at me. "Her name ain't *Estel*-avisham, Pip."

"A slip of the tongue," I said, but there was no fooling Joe. He pointed out that I had been paid off. My work there was done. Miss Havisham had been very clear that the twenty-five-guinea payment put an end to my visits to Satis House. It was sensible advice, which I was determined to ignore.

I begged Joe for a half day off. Joe, being Joe, granted it.

All might have been well but for Orlick.

Orlick also worked at Joe's forge. He was a surly man, always rude and resentful. If I was being given a half day off, Orlick said, why shouldn't he have one too?

Joe, being Joe, granted it.

And again, all might have been well but for my sister.

My sister, being my sister, made a fuss. She called Joe a fool and Orlick a crook. Orlick responded by calling my sister a shrew and all manner of other names, and the row grew so much that Joe felt compelled to defend his wife. It ended in a fight where Joe knocked Orlick down, and my sister fainted.

When the drama was over, I slipped away to Satis House, where I discovered that I really should have listened to Joe.

Estella was not there. She had gone abroad, Miss Havisham informed me with a nasty smile. She told me Estella was becoming an educated lady.

"Far out of your reach," Miss Havisham added. "Do you feel you have lost her?"

I knew not what to say, and she seemed to find my silence most amusing.

13

When I returned home, I found it in a state of uproar. While I had been at Satis House and Joe had been out, someone had attacked my sister. She had been struck from behind, knocked out cold by a blow to the back of her head.

I was sure Orlick was to blame, but the police could find no evidence and so Orlick stayed free.

My sister survived the attack, but she was changed by it. Her sight was affected, her hearing and memory damaged, and her speech too slurred to understand. Her temper was greatly improved, however.

Biddy – a childhood friend of mine – moved in with us to care for my sister. Home became a welcoming, restful place, but I was still ashamed of it.

I fell into a routine of apprentice life, but I could not forget Estella, and I could not keep away from Satis House. I paid another visit to Miss Havisham on my birthday. Again, Estella was not there, and the visit lasted only a few minutes. But at the end of it, Miss Havisham gave me a guinea and told me to come again next year on my birthday. It became an annual custom. Each year, nothing changed – not Miss Havisham, nor the house, nor Estella's absence.

But Biddy did.

Biddy grew up. She was pretty and kind and did not laugh at me even when I confided in her that I longed to become a gentleman. Biddy was fond of me, I knew. If I could have fallen in love with her, I might have been content. Happy, even. But memories of Estella kept hitting me like missiles. So did the thought that my sister had planted in my mind long ago: that one day Miss Havisham might "do something" for me.

14

It was the fourth year of my apprenticeship. A Saturday night. Joe and I were drinking in the local tavern when a London lawyer named Jaggers came in asking for the blacksmith, Joe Gargery.

Jaggers asked Joe, "You have an apprentice known as Pip? Is he here?"

"I am!" I cried before Joe had even opened his mouth.

Jaggers did not recognise me, but I knew him. There was no mistaking the smell of that expensive soap! He was the man who had grabbed me by the throat during my second visit to Satis House. Had he been sent here by Miss Havisham?

Jaggers said he wished to have a private conversation with us, so we all went home. Once there, Jaggers gave us extraordinary news.

I had "Great Expectations".

There was a secret benefactor. When I came of age, I would inherit a handsome property. Until then, I was to be removed from my life as an apprentice and to be given a gentleman's education. Jaggers suggested Matthew Pocket should be my tutor, a name I'd heard spoken at Miss Havisham's. Jaggers was to be my guardian, he said. He would give me money as and when I needed it. The only condition was that I ask no questions. Jaggers was forbidden to reveal my benefactor's name, and I was forbidden to ask it.

Arrangements were made; everything was settled. In a week's time, I was to be off to London to start my new life.

When Jaggers left the house, a great silence came down between Joe and me. I sat looking into the fire, and the more I stared at the flames, the less I felt able to speak.

At last, I went to my room. It was strange. I now had Great Expectations but felt sad and lonely and afraid. I crept into my bed but knew I'd never have the deep, sound sleep of a child there ever again.

15

The following morning, Joe put my apprenticeship papers in the fire.

I was free. I was wealthy. And so I behaved as foolishly as any young man who suddenly comes into money might do. I spent the money Jaggers had given me lavishly but not wisely. I ordered new clothes from the tailor and was fawned over and flattered. In my new attire, I went to visit Miss Havisham.

"I'm not surprised by this transformation," she said.

"Mr Jaggers told me all about it," she said.

"So, you have a secret benefactor?" she said.

"A promising future?" she said.

"You are to become a gentleman!"

Each sentence was delivered with a knowing twinkle in her eyes as if this was a great joke between us – another game Miss Havisham wanted me to play.

I was sure that she was my secret benefactor. And the question whispered in my head – did she mean to shape me into a suitable husband for Estella?

When it was time for me to go, Miss Havisham stretched out a hand, and I knelt before her and kissed it.

Then I left my fairy godmother standing in the dimly lit room beside the rotten bride cake that was hidden in cobwebs.

On my last evening at home, I dressed again in my new clothes. We had a hot supper of roast fowl, but it was an odd, awkward evening.

I left for London at five the following morning. I'd told Joe that I wished to walk away alone. Was I embarrassed to be seen with him? Yes. I felt a little guilty and a little ashamed, but I did it just the same.

The morning mists were rising from the marshes, I was going to London, and a whole new world was laid out at my feet.

THE SECOND STAGE OF PIP'S
GREAT EXPECTATIONS

16

The British are convinced that everything we have and everything we do is the very best in the world. If I had not held this view of British superiority, I might have found London to be grey, greasy, ugly, crooked, narrow and dirty.

The journey had taken five hours. Once I alighted from the stagecoach, I made my way to the address that Jaggers had given me. He was in court and so I had to wait in a gloomy room lit only by a skylight. When Jaggers returned, he was surrounded by clients – pitiful, ragged people all begging for his help. They reeked of desperation. No wonder he washed off their smell with such heavily scented soap!

Jaggers had arranged for me to stay with my tutor's son Herbert for a few days. On Monday, Herbert would take me to his father's house, which lay upriver in Hammersmith, where I would begin my gentleman's education. Mr Jaggers then handed me over to his clerk, a man called Wemmick. I had to follow him through the narrow streets to Herbert's rooms at Barnard's Inn.

The place suffered from dry rot, wet rot – every kind of rot. Smells of rat and mouse and beetle attacked my nostrils as I followed Wemmick up stairs that seemed to be slowly crumbling into sawdust.

Wemmick abandoned me on the top floor outside Herbert's rooms. Herbert was not in, so again I had to wait. After half an hour passed, I heard footsteps approaching.

Herbert was carrying bags of strawberries. He introduced himself and then explained that he thought I might like fruit after my dinner as I was from the countryside. As he wrestled to get his door open, he was fast turning the strawberries into jam. So I took the bags from him, and he went into battle with the door again. It surrendered so suddenly that Herbert was thrown back onto me. We both laughed.

And then we looked properly at one another and realised that we had met – and fought each other – years before.

"You're the prowling boy!" he exclaimed.

"And you," said I, "are the pale young gentleman!"

17

Herbert and I stood staring at each other, and again we both burst out laughing.

Herbert had ordered in dinner, and when it arrived, we sat and ate and talked. There was so little space in the room that the butter was placed on an armchair, the bread on the bookshelves, the cheese in the coal scuttle and the boiled fowl in my bed. As we ate, Herbert told me what he knew of Miss Havisham and Estella.

He'd been at Miss Havisham's on her birthday because, like me, he had been sent for. Like me, it had been vaguely suggested that Miss Havisham might "do something" for him. Like me, Herbert had wondered if Miss Havisham meant for him to become Estella's husband. But whatever Miss Havisham had planned for Herbert had come to nothing. Herbert said that Miss Havisham had clearly preferred me. While I had Great Expectations, Herbert had none.

That evening, Herbert told me some of Miss Havisham's history. Her mother had died when she'd been a baby, and her father had married again. Miss Havisham had a half-brother called Arthur. He had grown into such a very bad man that their father hadn't left Arthur any money when he died. Miss Havisham inherited everything. She became an extremely wealthy woman, and it was then that she fell wildly in love with a gentleman who claimed to be devoted to her. Herbert said it was very likely that this "gentleman" had plotted with her half-brother Arthur to ruin her.

Miss Havisham spoiled her beloved gentleman with gifts and money, and gave him anything he asked for. Herbert's father, Matthew Pocket, warned Miss Havisham against him, but she would not listen. In a rage, she'd ordered Matthew Pocket out of the house, and they had not seen each other since.

"The marriage day of Miss Havisham and her gentleman was fixed," Herbert concluded. "The gown ordered, the feast prepared. The day came, but not the bridegroom. He sent a letter—"

"Which Miss Havisham received when she was dressing for her marriage," I said. "At twenty minutes to nine?"

Herbert nodded. He didn't know what had happened to the gentleman and Arthur afterwards, or whether the two men were alive or dead.

The only certainty was that Miss Havisham had adopted Estella for one purpose only: to take her revenge on all men.

18

Mr Pocket's house in Hammersmith was a muddled sort of place, all noise and confusion. His wife didn't care what their seven children did or how their servants behaved as long as no one told her about it. From time to time, Mr Pocket reacted to the chaos by pushing his fingers into his hair and trying to lift himself above it all.

When I had been there two or three days, Mr Pocket and I had a long talk. Jaggers had told him that I was not destined for any kind of profession. The only reason I was being educated was so I could "hold my own" with other rich young gentlemen.

And so I began my studies. Mr Pocket was an energetic, honourable tutor, and so I became an energetic, honourable student. I applied myself fully to my books.

Meanwhile, Herbert taught me to behave in polite society. He did it all so tactfully that I was very grateful to him. He showed me how I should hold my knife and fork. He smoothed off my rough country edges and wiped away my working ways until I became perfectly presentable.

Besides myself, Mr Pocket had two other students living with him. Startop, whom I liked, and Bentley Drummle, whom I did not.

Drummle would become a baron one day, if the current heir ever did him the favour of dying. He was a gentleman by birth but not by nature. Drummle was a sullen, sulky fellow and a miserable student. He picked up every book resentfully, as if its writer had done him mortal injury. Idle, proud, suspicious, Drummle had been sent to Mr Pocket when he was a head taller and half a dozen heads thicker than most gentlemen.

I acquired a boat for myself, and Startop, Drummle and I often spent our evenings on the river. Sometimes Herbert would join us, but more often Startop and I would row homeward side by side, laughing and conversing from one boat to the other as we went.

Drummle would follow behind, silently sliding under the overhanging banks and among the rushes. Even when the tide would have carried him fast, he would creep along near the shore like some monstrous toad, coming after us in the dark backwater while Startop and I rowed in the moonlight midstream.

19

One morning, I received a letter from Biddy informing me that Joe would visit the next day. I was horrified. If I could have kept Joe away by paying him money, I would have done so.

Joe came to Barnard's Inn. I had developed a gentleman's expensive habits by then and had taken a half-share in Herbert's rooms. I spent a great deal of time there, just as Herbert spent a great deal of time with me at Hammersmith.

Herbert waited with me for Joe to arrive. I sat looking at the room. It was crammed with magnificent and expensive furniture I had bought for the place, but there was no hiding the sooty rain that fell outside the window or the smell of rats and rot that rose from the street. When I heard Joe climbing the stairs, I wanted to run away.

He came in, his face all shining, looking utterly absurd in his Sunday best. Joe was so very awkward and so very out of place.

Joe looked about our cramped rooms and said, "You two gentlemen, I hope you keep healthy in this spot. This may be a very good inn according to London folk, but I wouldn't keep a pig in it myself."

We had ordered food, and as we ate, I winced at Joe's table manners. He sometimes fell silent with his fork halfway to his mouth. He dropped more than he ate and then pretended that he hadn't.

Herbert was polite and kind to Joe, but I could barely bring myself to speak to him. I didn't realise that Joe's discomfort was my fault. If I had been easy with Joe, Joe would have been easy with me. But I was out of temper and embarrassed. I wanted Joe gone, and he knew it.

After a while, Herbert left us to go to the city. When Joe and I were alone, he revealed the reason for his visit. Miss Havisham had given him a message for me.

Estella had come home.

Estella wished to see me.

Message delivered, Joe stood up.

"Pip, dear old chap," Joe said slowly. "Life is made of ever so many partings. Divisions must come. You and me is not people to be together in London nor anywhere unless it be among friends. You shall never see me again in these clothes. I'm wrong in these clothes. I'm wrong out of the forge. Wrong out of the kitchen, wrong off the marshes. Come and see me there. You won't find half so much fault with me there."

He touched me gently on the forehead as he had done when I was small, then he left. Tears suddenly misted my eyes. I recovered myself a little and hurried after him, but Joe was gone.

.

20

I set off for Miss Havisham's. I would stay at Joe's the night before, I thought. I would put things right between us.

But when I reached my home town, I invented all manner of excuses. I told myself I was not expected at Joe's, my bed would not be ready, I would be in the way, Joe's was too far away from Miss Havisham's.

I stayed at the inn, and in the morning I was up and out and on my way to Satis House, imagining the brilliant future she had in mind for me.

Miss Havisham had adopted Estella and had as good as adopted me. I decided she must intend to bring us together. I would restore the bleak house, let sunshine into those dark rooms, set the clocks going, tear down the cobwebs, destroy the vermin. I would do all the shining deeds of a brave knight in a fairy tale and marry the beautiful princess.

For I loved Estella. I knew that I loved her against reason, against peace and hope and happiness and against all discouragement. I loved Estella simply because I had no choice. She was irresistible.

When I arrived, Miss Havisham was in the old chair by the old table in the old dress. Sitting near her was an elegant lady I thought I had never seen before. But then the lady lifted her head and looked at me. She had Estella's eyes. And at once I felt myself sliding backwards. I was a rough and common boy looking up at a glittering star.

Estella held out a hand, and I stammered a greeting.

"Is he changed?" Miss Havisham asked Estella with that greedy look of hers.

"Very much," said Estella.

"Less rough and common?" said Miss Havisham, playing with Estella's hair.

Estella laughed and looked at me, then laughed again. While we sat there in that strange room, I learned that Estella had been in France and was going to London. After speaking for a while, Miss Havisham sent us out to walk in the garden.

Estella and I strolled side by side until we came to the place where Herbert and I had fought.

Estella stopped and said, "What a strange creature I was back then! I saw the fight that day. I enjoyed it very much."

"Herbert and I are great friends now," I told her.

"And his father is your tutor? Since your change of fortune, you have changed your companions. Good. What was fit company for you once would be unfit now."

Any last thoughts I'd had of seeing Joe fled from my mind.

As we went on, we talked more of the past, but Estella remembered barely anything. She didn't recall that she'd let me kiss her nor that she'd made me cry.

"Things like that don't stay in my mind. You must know," Estella said, "that I have no heart."

"Impossible!" I replied.

"Oh, I have a heart to be stabbed in or shot. If it ceased to beat, I should cease to be. But I have no softness there, no sentiment, no tenderness. I will never bestow my heart on anyone because I do not have one to give."

At last, we went back to the house, and I pushed Miss Havisham in the wheeled chair round the old room. Time melted away until the dinner hour was close at hand and Estella left us to dress.

As she reached the door, Estella looked back, and Miss Havisham blew her a kiss with a hungry intensity that was dreadful to see.

Then Miss Havisham turned to me.

"Is she beautiful?" she asked. "Do you admire her?"

"Everybody who sees her must," I said.

Miss Havisham put her arm around my neck and drew me to her. "Love her, love her, love her. If she favours you, love her. If she wounds you, love her. If she tears your heart to pieces, love her, love her, love her!"

The muscles of her thin arm swelled as she clasped me with desperate eagerness.

"Hear me, Pip!" Miss Havisham went on. "I adopted her to be loved. I bred her and educated her to be loved. I made her what she is so she might be loved. Love her. Love her!"

Miss Havisham said it over and over. Coming from her lips, it sounded like a curse.

"What is love?" she said. "It is blind devotion, unquestioning self-humiliation, utter submission. Love is giving up your whole heart and soul to the one who destroys you – as I did!"

A wild cry burst from her lips, and then she rose up in her chair and clawed at the air as if she wanted to strike herself against the wall and fall down dead.

21

That night, Miss Havisham's words echoed in my ears.

"I do love her," I said to myself, repeating it hundreds of times into my pillow. "I love her, I love her!"

I was sure Miss Havisham meant me to marry Estella and that Estella knew it and had agreed to it. A burst of gratitude came upon me – the glittering star was destined for me who was once a humble blacksmith's boy. Yet when would Estella return my feelings? When would I awaken her silent and sleeping heart?

I thought myself a brave knight in shining armour. I thought my feelings for Estella were high and great and noble.

But I never thought there was anything low and small and ignoble in keeping away from Joe – for I knew Estella would despise him.

Only a day had passed since Joe had brought tears into my eyes. God forgive me! They had soon dried.

22

A few days after I had returned to London, I received a note.

It did not start "Dear Sir" or "Dear Pip" or "Dear Anything" but simply said:

> *I am to come to London the day after tomorrow by the midday coach. I believe it was decided that you should meet me? Miss Havisham has that impression and I write in obedience to it. She sends her regards.*

> *Yours, Estella*

I knew no peace or rest until the coach arrived, and after that I knew no peace either.

When Estella stepped down from the coach, she was more beautiful than she had ever been. Her manner to me was so kind I thought Miss Havisham had influenced her in my favour.

"I am going to Richmond," Estella told me. "I am to have a carriage and you are to take me. This is my purse – you are to pay with it. Oh, you must take it! We have no choice but to obey instructions, you and I."

I ordered a carriage. While Estella and I waited for it to be readied, we drank tea and I took care of her, as required.

"Where are you going in Richmond?" I asked.

"I am going to live with a lady who will take me about town and introduce me and show me off to people."

"I suppose you will enjoy being admired?" I asked.

"I suppose so," Estella said carelessly.

She asked how I fared at the Pockets', and I replied boldly, "Pleasantly. Or at least – as pleasantly as I can away from you."

Estella called me a silly boy but let me kiss her again, once more on the cheek. "And now you are to take me to Richmond," she said.

Estella spoke as if we were mere puppets, and yet she seemed content. As we journeyed to Richmond, she made herself pleasant, and yet I was not happy. I knew that for now Estella held my heart carefully in her hand, but she could as easily crush it and throw it away and feel no regret.

We passed by Newgate gaol, then through Hammersmith, and I pointed out where Mr Pocket lived. It was not far from Richmond, and I said I hoped I should see her sometimes.

"Oh yes," Estella replied. "You are to see me often. Miss Havisham has great plans, you know, Pip. I am to write to her constantly and report how I get on – I and the jewels."

We came to Richmond too soon. In moments, Estella was absorbed into the house, and I stood outside imagining how happy I would be if I lived there with her. Yet I knew in my heart that I was never happy with Estella, only ever miserable.

23

In the years that followed, I returned to the forge only once: on the day of my sister's funeral.

It was a ridiculously showy affair. Joe would have preferred a simple ceremony, with just a few friends carrying the coffin, but he had feared people would think that was lacking in respect. And so Joe wore a little black cloak tied in a large bow under his chin as we and a whole host of paid mourners paraded across the marshes to the church. There, my sister was laid in the earth alongside my father and mother and five little brothers while the larks sang high above our heads.

When the funeral and the feast were over, Joe and Biddy and I were left alone in the house. Joe was very much pleased when I asked if I might sleep in my old room, and I felt I had done a very gracious thing by bestowing my presence upon them.

When I left the following day, I shook Joe by the hand and promised I would be back soon and often. Biddy looked at me as if she did not believe a word of it.

And Biddy, of course, was right.

24

If Estella's house at Richmond should ever become haunted, it will surely be haunted by my ghost. My spirit roamed that place when she lived there! Wherever my body was, my spirit was always with Estella.

In that house, I suffered every kind of torture that Estella could inflict. She used me to make her many admirers jealous, but whenever we were alone, she was rude and aloof and seemed further away than ever.

There were endless parties and picnics and fetes, operas and concerts. I pursued Estella during them all. Life was a non-stop round of pleasures that were all misery to me.

One evening, Estella sent for me. We had been given instructions. Miss Havisham wished to see Estella and did not wish her to travel alone. I was to accompany her back to Satis House.

We were puppets. When Miss Havisham pulled our strings, we jumped to obey her command.

When we arrived, Miss Havisham seemed even more fond of Estella than she had been the last time I saw them together. There was something terrible in the energy of Miss Havisham's looks and embraces. She hung upon Estella's beauty as if she were devouring the creature she had reared.

Miss Havisham looked at me too with witch-like eagerness as she began demanding the names of Estella's admirers and how exactly they suffered at Estella's hands. I realised that Estella would only be permitted happiness when Miss Havisham's vengeful appetite had been satisfied.

Perhaps Estella had the same thought, for later that same day, sharp words were exchanged between the two women.

Miss Havisham was clutching Estella's hand while we were seated. Estella had always endured her fierce affection, but now she began to detach herself. At last, Estella rose and went to stand by the fire.

"Are you tired of me?" Miss Havisham demanded.

Estella looked at her with indifference, and Miss Havisham recoiled and exclaimed, "You have a cold, cold heart!"

Estella's graceful figure and beautiful face expressed nothing. Calmly she answered, "I am what you have made me."

With sudden distress, Miss Havisham called her thankless. Cruel.

Estella wasn't at all troubled. She remained calm and composed. "You have been very good to me, and I owe you everything. What do you want from me?"

"Love!" cried Miss Havisham.

"You ask me to give you what you never gave me," Estella said simply. "I cannot do the impossible."

"So proud! So hard!" Miss Havisham said. She was distraught now, tearing at her hair with both hands.

"Who taught me to be proud? Who taught me to be hard? Who praised me when I learned my lessons? It was you who made me this way."

I left them then, with Miss Havisham on the floor and Estella still standing like a statue by the fire. I walked in the starlight for an hour or so.

When I returned, they had reconciled, and Estella was sitting once more beside Miss Havisham.

The ill feeling did not return that night or on any of our later visits. Everything went on much as before, and yet I noticed that sometimes Miss Havisham looked at Estella and seemed afraid.

25

If I could write Estella's story without mentioning
Bentley Drummle, I would gladly do so. Sadly, it is
impossible.

Bentley Drummle had finished his studies
and returned to his family hole. But as he was a
member of the same gentlemen's club as Herbert
and Startop and myself, it was impossible to avoid
him altogether.

At the end of a meal, it was the custom for
club members to drink a toast to a lady. One night
it was Drummle's turn, and he raised a glass to
"Estella!"

I was furious hearing her name in his mouth. I
accused him of not knowing her, of having no right
to toast her. We had all of us had a great deal to
drink, and a row broke out. Every club member
joined in with enthusiasm.

Blood might have been spilled; a duel might
have been fought. Instead, it was agreed that

if Drummle could bring evidence from Estella that they knew each other, then I would have to apologise to him.

The next evening, Drummle arrived at the club bearing a polite little note from Estella saying that she did indeed know him and had had the honour of dancing with him several times.

Drummle became one of Estella's admirers. Our paths crossed often, and never happily. She toyed with him, as she toyed with all of them.

One night, I said to her in some distress, "You give Drummle looks and smiles that you never give to me!"

When Estella answered, she was unusually serious, "Do you want me to deceive and entrap you?"

"Do you deceive and trap him, Estella?" I said.

"Yes. And many others. I deceive and trap all of them but you. You are different."

I had to be content with that, yet I could not be easy. There was something about Drummle that I feared. He did not watch Estella the way other admirers watched her, with a look of dazed enchantment in his eyes. He watched her patiently. Steadily. Coldly calculating. He was like a toad, squatting in his hole, waiting for his prey to come.

26

Time passed. When I came of age, I expected the name of my benefactor to be revealed, but all that happened was that I was given an income of £500 a year. It was a generous sum, but one that I always overspent.

While I sank deeper into debt, Herbert's career flourished. I had some part in that, but I will not go into the details in these pages. I must move my story on to a wet, stormy evening when Herbert was away in France on business, and I sat alone reading.

I was twenty-three years old by then, and we had long since moved from Barnard's Inn to rooms at the Temple. Just as the clock struck eleven, I heard footsteps on the stairs. I knew the lights there had been blown out by the wind, so carried my lantern to the top of the stairwell and called, "Is there someone there?"

"Yes," said a voice from the darkness.

"Who do you want?" I asked.

"Mr Pip."

"That's me. What's the matter?"

"Nothing."

I stood with my lantern held over the stair-rail as the man appeared. Dressed like a voyager at sea, he was a complete stranger. Yet he seemed delighted to see me. He said he had come on businesss, and so I invited him in reluctantly.

He looked about the rooms with pride and pleasure, almost as if he owned the place, and then he held out both hands towards me. I half suspected he was mad, so I was reluctant to take them. Of course he noticed and was hurt by my reaction.

"It's disappointing," he said. "Having looked forward to this for so long and having come so far. But you're not to blame. Give me half a minute."

He sat down on a chair, and as I stared, the realisation slowly dawned that I knew him.

This was the convict. The man from the graveyard, the man who had fought in the muddy ditch. He was sitting in my chair before my fire! Again, he held out both his hands, and this time I took them.

"You acted kindly back then, my boy," the convict said. "I have never forgot it!"

I felt nothing but horror. Disgust. I took my hands from his and said coolly, "I hope you have shown your gratitude by mending your way of life. Thanking me is not necessary. You must understand that—"

"What?" he interrupted. "What must I understand?"

I tried again. "I am glad you have come to thank me. But our ways are different ways. I am a gentleman now. I do not wish to renew our ..." I hesitated, not knowing what to call our relationship. I said instead, "You are wet and weary. Will you drink something before you go?"

He nodded, so I mixed hot rum and water. As I handed it to him, his eyes filled with tears.

"I am sorry I spoke harshly," I said. "I truly wish you well and happy. How are you living?"

He told me a little about himself. His name was Magwitch, he said. Not long after our first encounter, he had been sent to New South Wales in Australia. Magwitch had served his term as a convict and then farmed sheep and taken up all kinds of trades. He had done wonderfully well for himself and was now a very rich man.

He looked at me very directly and said, "You was a poor boy once. May I ask how you have done so well since you and me was out on those lonely marshes?"

Magwitch's look was so steady and contained so much meaning that I began to tremble. Stuttering, I said I had been chosen to inherit some property.

"Might I ask what property?" he said.

"I don't know," I replied.

"Might I ask whose property?"

"I don't know."

"Could I make a guess at the income you've had since you come of age?" Magwitch said. "The first figure. Might it be a five?"

I stared at him and gave no answer.

"There must have been a guardian who made the arrangements," he said. "A lawyer, maybe. As to the first letter of his name, might it be a J?"

The truth hit me in a flash. I struggled for breath. I could not speak. The room began to spin, and he caught me, set me on the sofa like a child and propped me on cushions. Then he knelt before me, his face close to mine.

"Yes, Pip. It's my doing. I've made a gentleman of you! The first guinea I ever earned I swore would go to you. I swore that if I got rich, you would get rich. I lived rough so you could live smooth. I worked hard so you did not have to. I could never be a gentleman, but by God I could make one."

I shrank from him as if he was some terrible beast, but in his joy he seemed not to notice.

"Pip, I'm your second father," Magwitch said. "You're my son. I've put away money only for you. Look at you, dear boy! A gentleman! Didn't you never think it might be me who done it?"

"Never! Never! Never!" I shouted.

Worse was to come. As Magwitch talked more, I began to understand the terrible risk he had taken in crossing the world to see me. He had been sent to Australia for the rest of his life. He was meant to die there, not to return to England! If he was caught here, he would be hanged. Once more he had put his life in my hands.

It was a crushing responsibility. Even worse was the knowledge that I had lied to myself. Miss Havisham's plans for Estella and I were nothing but my own foolish imaginings.

I didn't know what crimes Magwitch had committed. But I had seen him attacking that second convict with fury. I feared him. Magwitch slept in Herbert's room that night, and when I heard his snores, I locked his door before I tried to sleep myself.

I woke at five. The candles were burned out, the fire was dead and the wind and rain lashed in the black darkness.

THE THIRD STAGE OF PIP'S GREAT EXPECTATIONS

27

I groped around in the darkness at five o'clock that
morning as I tried and failed to find the means to
light a candle. At last, I decided to ask the porter
for help. I groped my way down the staircase but
stumbled over a man who had been crouching in
the corner. He fled before I could ask who he was
and what he had been doing there.

Was he a beggar, sheltering from the storm?
Or had Magwitch been followed?

Once I had found a light, I sat in a chair
dozing until Magwitch woke. He ate breakfast
like a hungry old dog. Noisily. Greedily. I was so
repelled by the sight of him I ate nothing at all.

Magwitch was convinced he wasn't in danger.
The only people who knew he was here were myself
and Jaggers, he said. Even if he happened to meet
an old acquaintance, no one would recognise him.
Besides, he told me that whatever the risk, he would

still have come back. He had to see the gentleman he had made of me.

I could not feel easy, and so I made plans to keep Magwitch safe. He must be disguised, I knew. He would need a haircut. New clothes. I used that as an excuse and went out to make purchases for him. I also went to see Jaggers.

"I want to know if what I have been told is true," I demanded.

Jaggers knew exactly why I had come. But Jaggers was a lawyer. For him, words were weapons. They could preserve life or they could kill.

He said, "What you've been *told*, Pip? Or *informed*? Choose carefully. *Told* implies a verbal communication, and that isn't likely from a man who is in New South Wales."

I understood his meaning at once. We needed to be very careful. "*Informed*," I said. "*Informed*."

And so we edged very carefully around the subject. Gradually, Jaggers confirmed the truth of all that Magwitch had said.

*

For five days, Magwitch and I were alone together in my rooms. For those five days, I seemed locked in a nightmare – a sort of reverse *Frankenstein*. It wasn't that I had made a monster who was in pursuit of me. No ... Magwitch was my creator, and I was his creature, and he was delighted with me. And the more he admired me, the fonder he became of me, the more I was repelled by him.

28

After five days, Herbert came back from France, bursting in and delighted to be home. Then he saw Magwitch, and his expression changed.

Herbert was a true and loyal friend. When I explained the situation, he did not question that we should keep Magwitch secret or that the man should be helped to get away. While Magwitch slept, the two of us began to make a plan.

Herbert and I were both certain that Magwitch should get out of England for his own safety. We were also certain that he would not go unless I went with him, given the man was so fond of me. I had no choice in the matter.

However, it was uncertain how we were to get Magwitch away unseen, and where the two of us were to go. Every night, Herbert and I talked and talked and tried to plan a future. And every day, little by little, Magwitch told us something of his past life.

I have already said that my tale involves many people and many events, and that they were the scattered pieces of a jigsaw puzzle in the beginning.

I was now in the third stage of my Great Expectations, and as my life fell apart, the pieces of the puzzle began to come together.

This was the first. Magwitch told Herbert and I that he had no idea where he'd been born or who his parents were. His earliest memory was of stealing turnips. Magwitch was a ragged, starved child, who made his way tramping, begging, thieving – surviving as best he could.

And then he met Compeyson, who was a gentleman, but a gentleman similar to Bentley Drummle. Compeyson was a well-bred, wealthy villain.

In the past, Compeyson had worked with another gentleman villain named Arthur. They'd had huge success plotting against a rich lady, stealing half her money and all her mind. When Arthur became ill, Compeyson took on Magwitch to do his dirty work, but Magwitch was no partner in his crime. He was Compeyson's underling, always in debt to his master, always under his thumb – always working, never getting free.

At last, Magwitch and Compeyson were arrested for their crimes and brought to trial. But Magwitch was made to look like a common criminal while Compeyson looked like a noble gentleman who had been led astray. Compeyson got off lightly, but the law came down heavily on Magwitch. Compeyson was sentenced to seven years, but Magwitch was given fourteen. So, that day on the marshes, Magwitch could not bear to let Compeyson escape. By that point in his story, it had also become clear to both Herbert and me that Compeyson was also the man who had destroyed Miss Havisham.

I could not blame Magwitch for attacking Compeyson in that ditch. In his place, I would have done the same.

29

I was to leave England, but first I had to see Estella.

I made my way to Richmond but found she had gone to Satis House without me. So I followed her there uninvited.

I found Estella in the room where the dressing table stood and the wax candles burned. Amid all that ruin, Estella was sitting on a cushion at Miss Havisham's feet, knitting.

Recent events had changed me. I did not enter that room as I had so many times before – meekly, humbly, so very grateful to Miss Havisham for all I supposed she had done for me. I was angry. Distressed. In need of answers.

Estella kept her eyes down and carried on knitting, but Miss Havisham looked steadily at me, confused by what she saw.

"What wind blows you here, Pip?" she asked.

"Miss Havisham," I said, "I went to Richmond yesterday and found Estella was here. It will not surprise you to know that I am as unhappy as you can have ever meant to make me. I have found out who my patron is. It is not a happy discovery, but I can say no more – it is not my secret."

I paused for a moment, then asked, "When you first brought me here ... was it as a paid servant, simply to do as you pleased?"

Miss Havisham nodded.

"Mr Jaggers—" I said.

"Mr Jaggers," Miss Havisham interrupted me, "had nothing to do with it. It is pure coincidence that he is my lawyer and also the lawyer of your patron."

"But when I fell into that mistake, you led me on," I said. "You knew what I thought – what I imagined – and you never corrected me."

"Yes," she said.

"Was that kind?" I asked.

"Kind?" Miss Havisham struck her walking stick upon the ground. "Why should I be kind? You made your own snares!"

I turned to Estella. I tried to command my trembling voice as I said, "You know I have loved you long and dearly."

Estella raised her eyes and looked at me unmoved. She didn't stop knitting. Miss Havisham glanced from me to her and her to me.

"I should have said this sooner, Estella," I went on. "My mistake about my benefactor led me to hope that Miss Havisham meant us for one another. I know now that I shall never call you mine. I know not what my future will be, or where I may go. But still I love you. I have loved you ever since I first saw you."

Estella shook her head as she looked at me and carried on knitting, but I pressed on.

"If Miss Havisham had known what she did, I would say it was cruel of her to torture me. But suffering such pain herself, Miss Havisham could not see mine."

Miss Havisham put her hand to her heart and held it there.

Estella said calmly, "It seems there are sentiments which I cannot understand. I don't care. I have tried to warn you, have I not?"

"Yes," I said miserably. "I hoped you didn't mean it. You are so young, so beautiful – it is not natural to have no feelings!"

"It is natural for me," said Estella. "It is the way I was shaped."

My thoughts turned to Bentley Dummle. I'd heard rumours that he planned to marry Estella, but I hadn't thought them true, for surely she would refuse him?

"I hear Bentley Drummle is courting you," I said. "You cannot love him?"

"What have I told you?" Estella said angrily. "I cannot love. Do you still think I don't mean what I say?"

"You wouldn't marry him, Estella?" I said.

Estella looked at Miss Havisham, then said, "Why not tell you the truth? I am going to be married to him."

I dropped my face into my hands. In that moment, I blamed Miss Havisham. Estella was only a puppet, obeying her commands.

"Estella, don't let Miss Havisham lead you into this! Not Drummle! Miss Havisham gives you to him in order to hurt all the better men who truly love you. Take one of them if you will not take me!"

It seemed that my earnestness awoke something in her. If she could have felt compassion, she would have done so then.

"I am going to be married to him," Estella said gently. "It is my choice to do so."

"Your choice? To fling yourself away upon a brute?" I said.

"On whom should I fling myself away? On a good man who loves me, who would soon discover I can feel nothing in return? Drummle is my choice. Miss Havisham would prefer me not to marry anyone, but I am tired of the life I have led. I wish to change it. Say no more. We will never understand each other."

"He is such a brute!" I said.

"Well, I will be no blessing to him."

"How can I see you Drummle's wife?"

"It will pass. You will get me out of your thoughts in a week."

"Out of my thoughts?" I replied. "You are part of my existence, part of myself. You have been in every line I have ever read, everything I have ever seen – the river, the sails of the ships, the marshes, the clouds, the light, the darkness, in the wind, in the woods, in the sea, in the streets. Your presence is everywhere in my life, Estella, and will be to my last hour. You will be part of me for ever, despite separating here and now. God bless you; God forgive you!"

These broken words fell from my mouth like blood gushing from a wound. I kissed her hand, holding it to my lips for a few lingering moments.

And then I left. Estella watched me go without emotion. But Miss Havisham seemed full of pity and regret as she sat with her hand still covering her heart.

I walked all the way back to London.

When I reached my chambers, the night porter handed me an envelope. Words were scrawled across the front in Wemmick's writing: "READ THIS HERE".

Inside, a scrap of paper.

Three words:

DON'T GO HOME.

30

DON'T GO HOME – DON'T GO HOME – DON'T GO HOME.

The words banged in my skull as I fled along the street.

DON'T GO HOME – DON'T GO HOME – DON'T GO HOME.

I hailed a hackney carriage. I found a hostel in Covent Garden where rooms could be had even at that time of night.

DON'T GO HOME – DON'T GO HOME – DON'T GO HOME.

I lay in bed, but I could not sleep.

In the morning, I went to Wemmick.

I should explain that Wemmick was a man of two personalities. The one that worked as clerk to Mr Jaggers was cold and efficient. But the other one was a very different creature.

The Wemmick that went home at the end of the day was warm-hearted and kind and devoted to the care of his aged father. It was to that Wemmick that I went for help.

Magwitch's name was not mentioned by either of us. We referred only to my "uncle" who was "visiting me from the country". Wemmick had learned from his criminal contacts that my chambers had been watched. He had also learned that Compeyson was not only alive but in London, and that Compeyson was well aware that Magwitch had returned.

It seemed that Compeyson was determined to destroy him.

31

The moment Wemmick heard about Compeyson's plan to destroy Magwitch, he had gone to my chambers. But I was away, at Satis House, so Wemmick managed to warn Herbert that it would be wise to get my "uncle" away from there. Herbert had done so. Bless him!

I stayed at Wemmick's until after dark. And then I went to the house where Magwitch was in hiding and Herbert was keeping him company.

We sat. We talked. We made plans.

I would buy a new boat. Herbert and I would start rowing on the river again, as we had done when I lodged with his father. We would become so familiar a sight that no one would remark on it when the time came for us to get Magwitch downriver and onto a steamer headed for foreign shores.

Wemmick had promised to keep his ear to the ground. If he learned that Compeyson was going out of London for a while, he would send us a message. That would be the time for my "uncle" and me to take our voyage overseas.

32

It was while we were waiting that a second piece of the jigsaw puzzle began to fall into place.

I had been out in the boat that day and was strolling up into Cheapside. A large, soap-scented hand was suddenly laid upon my arm, and Jaggers said, "Come dine with me."

I was about to refuse, but Jaggers added, "Wemmick is coming." And so I went.

Dinner was an odd, uncomfortable affair. Jaggers' housekeeper was an unsettled woman who laid dishes before us with shaking hands and watchful eyes. Our conversation was no more restful. As we ate, Jaggers informed me that Miss Havisham wished to see me as soon as possible. And then he told me that Estella had become Drummle's wife. Jaggers predicted that their home would be a battleground.

"The stronger of them will win in the end," he said. "If it comes down to a battle of intellect,

Estella will be the victor. But Drummle has physical strength, and he may well use it."

Jaggers poured wine for the three of us and raised his glass. "Here's to Mrs Bentley Drummle. May the war end in her favour!"

His housekeeper was at his elbow, setting a dish upon the table. She withdrew her hands from it and stepped back, her fingers twitching nervously as if she was knitting. Her fingers moved in exactly the same pattern as Estella's had done ...

I stared at the housekeeper, transfixed. She had Estella's eyes. Estella's hands. The resemblance was extraordinary! Was she Estella's mother?

I said nothing until the meal was done and I was out on the street walking home alongside Wemmick.

After some pressing, Wemmick told me that Jaggers' housekeeper had been tried for the murder of a woman some twenty years before. Jaggers had been her lawyer, and he had tied the jury in such knots that she had walked free. She had been his housekeeper ever since.

At the time of the murder, the woman's child had also disappeared. She was suspected of killing it, but no body had ever been found.

33

The following day, I returned to Satis House. The place had changed now Estella had gone from it.

Miss Havisham was sitting on the hearth right beside the fire, looking into the flames with an air of utter loneliness. When she turned and her eyes rested on me, she asked, "Are you real?"

I realised whatever had remained of Miss Havisham's mind was shattered.

She handed me a book and whispered, "My name is there. Look! If you can ever write under my name 'I forgive her', do it, even if it is long after I am dead."

"Oh, Miss Havisham," I replied. "I can do it now. My life has been a thankless one. I have made so many mistakes! I want forgiveness far too much myself to be bitter with you."

Miss Havisham wept.

"What have I done?" she repeated over and over.

I knew not how to answer. She had indeed done terrible things. She had made her mind diseased – by shutting out the light, by hiding away from anything that might heal her. She'd taken a child and moulded her into an instrument of revenge. How could I find words of comfort for that?

"I did not know what I was doing!" Miss Havisham whispered. "When Estella came to me, I meant no more than to save her from a life of misery. But as she grew and grew so beautiful, I did worse. I stole her heart away and put ice in its place."

"Whose child was she?" I asked.

"I don't know. I only told Jaggers I wanted a little girl to rear and love. One night he brought her here, fast asleep. I named her Estella."

"What was her age then?" I asked.

"Two or three. Estella knows nothing about it."

At last, I got up to leave. Knowing I would never return to Satis House, I turned when I reached the door to the dining room and looked back.

At that moment, a great flaming light sprang up. Miss Havisham ran at me screaming as fire blazed all about her.

I wrapped her in my coat and dragged the cloth from the table so that the great heap of rottenness

fell to the floor. I rolled with Miss Havisham,
beating at the flames until they were all out.

34

Miss Havisham lived, but only just. She could not last long. As for me – both my hands and one arm were so badly burned, I could not look after myself. Herbert took care of me, and he also spent hours with Magwitch, talking with him and learning more of his story.

It was then that a third piece of the puzzle fell into place.

It seemed that long ago, Magwitch had been married to a young woman. They had a child – a little girl – whom he loved dearly.

The child's mother, Magwitch's wife, was very beautiful but very jealous and very revengeful. She murdered the woman she took to be her rival. That same night, she went to Magwitch and swore she would kill their child and that he would never see his little girl again.

He grieved for his lost daughter, yet he did not wish to see his wife hanged. Magwitch kept himself hidden until the trial was over so he would not be called on to give evidence against his wife.

And Compeyson used that fact against Magwitch to keep him in debt and work him harder.

This had all happened twenty years ago, some three or four years before Magwitch and I met in the graveyard. He told Herbert that I had reminded him of his lost child, who would have been the same age as I was then.

"Herbert," I said when the tale was done. "Touch my forehead. Am I feverish? Am I out of my mind?"

"No," said Herbert, after examining me. "You are quite yourself."

"Then the man we have in hiding down the river is Estella's father," I said.

35

I could not rest until all the pieces of the puzzle were put together. I went to Jaggers and told him I had learned something about Estella's background.

"But it seems I know more about it than Miss Havisham. I know Estella's mother," I said.

"Mother?" Jaggers repeated.

"I have seen her mother very recently. As have you."

"Yes?" said Jaggers.

"Perhaps I know more of Estella's history than even you do," I went on. "I know her father too. A man from New South Wales."

"Does he make this claim?" Jaggers asked.

"No. He doesn't know his daughter is alive."

It took more prodding and pleading, but Jaggers at last told me what I wished to know.

"Suppose that a lawyer was representing a woman accused of murder," Jaggers said. "She had told him she had hidden her child but not killed it. Suppose that same lawyer had been asked to find a child for an eccentric lady to love and look after and bring up. The lawyer worked among evil people and saw their evil deeds each day. He had seen countless children destroyed – imprisoned, whipped, transported, abandoned. And here was one little child out of all that heap who could be saved from it. And so that lawyer told his client to give the child she'd hidden to him. If she did that, the lawyer said he would do his best to get the women acquitted. Suppose all this was done. And the woman's wits had been so shaken by the terror of everything that when she emerged back into the world, she was scared and confused and broken. So, the lawyer took the woman in and gave her a roof over her head. Pip, imagine that the child grew up and became a married woman. Imagine that her mother and father both still lived. Would you reveal that secret?"

I looked at Wemmick, who held a finger to his lips as if to shush a small child.

I nodded. I understood.

I would keep what I had learned to myself.

36

On Monday evening, I received a note from Wemmick:

Wednesday is the day to do it.

I showed the note to Herbert and then put it in the fire.

We stared at each other, a question hanging in the air between us.

My hands had been so badly burned that I could not row the boat. How could we get Magwitch to safety now?

"Startop," Herbert suggested. "He's a good man, a skilled hand and fond of us. We don't need to tell him everything. We need only to say that there is an urgent reason for getting Magwitch away. You still plan to go with him?"

"Yes," I replied.

"Where?"

I didn't care as long as it was out of England. We would board any steamer bound for foreign shores that came our way. Gravesend would be crawling with people searching for Magwitch if anyone suspected he had fled, but if we could get him past there in our little boat, we would stand a good chance.

Steamers would leave London at high tide. If we could get downriver well before then, we could find a quiet spot to wait.

There was much work to be done before Wednesday, many things to be put in place. But our plan was made. We could only pray that it would work.

37

Wednesday was one of those March days when the sun shines hot and the wind blows cold. A day when it is summer in the light and winter in the shade.

Herbert and Startop and I stood on the river steps that morning as if not quite decided about whether to go on the water. After our pretence of indecision, we went on board and cast off. They rowed; I steered.

We knew the tide would begin to run down at nine and it would carry us along until three. After the tide had turned, we would row against the current until dark. By then, we should have come to the long reaches beyond Gravesend where the river was broad, the inhabitants few and the public houses isolated. We could seek one for our resting place that night.

The steamers would start from London at nine the following morning. We would hail the first steamer, and if we were not taken aboard, we would try another.

The crisp air, the sunlight and the relief of being on our way at last filled me with hope. We'd soon passed old London Bridge and Billingsgate Market, the Tower and Traitor's Gate. And there at last were the steps where Magwitch waited for us, looking so much like a river pilot that surely no one would think he was anything else?

I was truly delighted to see him.

"Dear boy!" Magwitch said as he settled down into the boat. "Faithful, dear boy, well done. Thankee. Thankee."

We rowed in and out among the shipping, the bobbing buoys, the flotsam and jetsam carried by the tide. At last, we reached a clearer stretch of river.

I looked all the time for signs that we were followed but saw none.

Magwitch was the least anxious of any of us. If danger came, he would meet it. But until then, he would not trouble himself with thoughts of what might happen.

"If all goes well," I said, "you will be free and safe in a few hours."

"I hope so," Magwitch replied.

"And think so?"

He dipped his hand in the water and said, smiling, "I think so. But we can no more see what will come in the next few hours than we can see to the bottom of this river. We can no more hold the tide than I can hold this handful of water."

Magwitch put his pipe in his mouth and sat smoking. He was composed and content as the tide ran strong and carried us past transport ships and emigrant ships. The river dropped lower and lower, but the tide was still with us as we passed Gravesend.

Soon the tide slackened, and the craft lying at anchor began to swing around. Ships taking advantage of the change in tide to get towards London started to crowd in on us.

We stayed near the shore. It was harder work now to row, but Herbert and Startop kept on until the sun began to set. We agreed to stop at the first lonely tavern we could find.

As it grew darker, we all began to feel that we were being followed. We were startled by anything: the slap of a wave against the boat or the flutter of a bird in the marshes.

Finally, we came to a tavern, and we went ashore for the night. We ate, we sat by the fire and then the only other customer in the place began to talk.

He asked if we'd seen a galley of four oars going up with the tide. He said he didn't like the look of it. The men rowing it had made him suspicious. They were not, he said, who they seemed. He was sure they were Customs Officers in pursuit of smugglers, but whatever the truth of it, it made the four of us uneasy.

The following day we rowed out to wait for the steamers. It was half past one when we saw the smoke of a steamer and behind it that of a second. Both were coming on at full speed, so Magwitch and I got ourselves ready to leave. We had just said our goodbyes to Herbert and Startop when a galley with four oars shot out from under a bank and rowed alongside us.

The first steamer was coming head-on very fast when the galley hailed us.

"You have a man there by the name of Magwitch," someone shouted out. "I call on him to surrender."

The galley rammed into the side of us.

I heard shouts from the steamer and heard the order on board to stop the paddles. The order was obeyed, but the steamer still came on. The steersman of the galley had put his hand on Magwitch, and both boats were swinging around. In the same moment, I saw Magwitch lean across and pull the cloak away from a man sitting hunched low in the galley.

It was Compeyson. The second convict I had seen all those years ago. He tilted backwards, utter terror on his familiar face as a great cry came from the steamer.

There was a crack! A splash! The boat sank under me.

I was plucked from the water and dragged into the galley. Herbert was there. So was Startop. But our boat and the two convicts were gone.

The steamer moved on, blowing furiously. The galley pulled away and then paused as we all looked at the water in silence. Presently, a dark object rose to the surface.

Magwitch! Swimming, but not swimming freely. Was he hurt? The moment he was pulled on board, he was handcuffed and his ankles chained.

The second steamer passed.

We waited and watched for Compeyson to bob up.

He did not.

We returned to the tavern. Magwitch was injured. He had gone under the steamer and been struck on the head as he rose. An injury to his chest had been from the galley. He and Compeyson had gone down fighting, and there had been a fierce struggle between them under the water.

Herbert and Startop returned to London by land, but Magwitch and I remained at the tavern until the tide turned. Then Magwitch was led down to the galley and put on board and I took my place by his side. I did not intend to move from there while Magwitch still lived.

Any disgust that I'd ever felt towards him had long since melted away. I now saw only a man who had tried to help me, who had been affectionate, grateful and generous towards me during all these years. I only saw in him a much better man than I had ever been to Joe.

38

Magwitch was taken to the police court the following day. He would have been taken to trial immediately had there been anyone who could confirm his identity. Compeyson had been meant to do it. It turned out that Compeyson himself had spread the rumour that he was going away from London for a while. It had been done to lure Magwitch out of hiding and into Compeyson's trap. But he was now dead and tumbling in the tides.

I had engaged Jaggers to act on Magwitch's behalf, and Jaggers would neither confirm nor deny Magwitch's identity. So, an old officer of the prison ship Magwitch had escaped from was sent for.

It delayed things, that was all. It could not change them.

The old officer came and identified Magwitch. He was to stand trial in a month.

During that time of waiting, Herbert came home one evening and said, "I fear I have to leave you."

Work was to take Herbert to Cairo.

He disliked going in my time of need, he said, but I put his mind at rest. Herbert then asked if I had planned what I would do in the future.

The future?

A difficult question to answer.

I knew that my Great Expectations had turned to dust, though I never told Magwitch this. When he was convicted, all his property would be forfeit to the Crown.

It meant I was penniless. Worse than penniless. I was deeply in debt. So, what was I to do? I had been given a gentleman's education. I had not learned a trade. I was an idle, useless creature, fit for nothing!

I said none of this to Herbert.

But Herbert said to me as tactfully and gently as he had once corrected my table manners that in time he would be delighted if I joined him in Cairo and worked as his clerk.

We shook hands on the arrangement. We parted on the Saturday of that same week, Herbert full of bright hopes, I full of dark despair.

39

Magwitch lay in the prison infirmary very ill. He had broken two ribs, and they had wounded his lungs. He breathed with pain and difficulty. I saw him every day but was allowed to stay only a short time. Magwitch spoke very little, and I watched him become slowly weaker.

It was a bright April day when the trial came, when drops of rain on the windows of the court glittered in the rays of the sun.

The trial was very short and very clear. Magwitch had become a reformed character, it was declared. He had lived honestly and profitably in New South Wales. But nothing could undo the fact that he had returned to England.

Magwitch was guilty as charged.

Magwitch was sentenced to death.

Magwitch had been allowed to sit in a chair during his trial. They wished him to stay alive until his execution.

I hoped and prayed that he would die before that day came.

Yet suppose he did not? That night I began to write a petition to the Home Secretary. When it was finished and sent in, I wrote other petitions to other men in authority. I even penned one to the Crown itself. I did not rest, only sleeping at my desk. After the petitions were sent in, I paced the streets.

My daily visits to Magwitch had been shortened, and I was closely watched. I think they suspected that I would carry poison to him.

The days went on and Magwitch became very quiet. Sometimes he could not speak at all and would only communicate with a slight squeeze of my hand. After ten days had passed, I saw an even greater change in him. When I went in, his eyes were turned towards the door and lit up as I entered.

"Dear boy," Magwitch said. "I feared you were late. But I knew you couldn't be. You always wait at the gate, don't you?"

"Yes, I do," I said. "So as not to lose a moment of the time."

"Thankee. God bless you! You've never deserted me."

He lay on his back, breathing with great difficulty.

"Are you in much pain today?" I asked.

"I don't complain of none, dear boy."

"You never do."

Magwitch had spoken his last words. He smiled, took my hand and held it to his chest. Our allotted time had run out, but when I looked round, the governor of the prison was there. He whispered, "You needn't go yet."

I thanked him and said, "Might I speak to him alone, if he can hear me?"

The governor stepped back and beckoned the officer away.

And I said, "Dear Magwitch, I must tell you something. You understand what I say?"

He replied with a gentle pressure on my hand.

"You had a child once, whom you loved and lost."

The pressure on my hand grew stronger.

"She lived and found powerful friends," I said. "She is living now. She is a lady, and I love her!"

With a last faint effort, Magwitch raised my hand to his lips. Then he gently let it sink upon his chest again and breathed his last.

40

I was all alone. Maybe I would have gone to Cairo then if I'd been able to pay the fare. But I could not. If I hadn't been falling ill, I would have been seriously alarmed about my debts.

For a day or two, I lay on the sofa or on the floor – wherever I happened to sink down. Then one night I suffered dreams full of anxiety and horror, and in the morning when I tried to sit up, I could not do so. I dreamed again, and when I woke, there were two men staring at me.

"What do you want?" I mumbled.

"Well, sir," replied one of the men, "you're arrested. You owe a debt of a hundred and twenty-three pounds, fifteen and six. You're to come with me."

But I could not get up. I could not move. I do not know if they tried to take me, for I recall nothing else.

I had a terrible fever and lived in nightmares. For days, weeks, they were vast and terrifying. I was haunted by the distorted faces of people who transformed from one thing to another. But as time passed, it seemed that all these horrid transformations changed. They settled down into the likeness of Joe.

And one morning there he was, in my rooms, sitting on my window seat smoking his pipe.

"Joe?" I said. "Is it you?"

"It is, old chap." Joe's voice cracked with delight and relief.

"Oh, Joe, you break my heart!" I said. "Look angry at me. Strike me. Rage at my lack of gratitude. Don't be good to me!"

Joe had his arm about me, and he said, "Dear old Pip, old chap. You and me have always been the best of friends. And when you're well enough to go out – what larks we shall have!"

He moved over to the window again and stood with his back to me, wiping his eyes.

"How long, Joe?" I asked.

"You mean how long has your illness lasted?"

"Yes."

"It's the end of May, Pip. Tomorrow is the first of June."

"Have you been here the whole time?" I said.

"Pretty much. News of your being ill was brought by letter. And Biddy said, 'Go to him, without a minute's loss of time.' And so I came and here I stayed and here I am still."

I got better slowly. And while Joe stayed with me, I felt I was a child again. He sat and talked to me with his old confidence and simplicity. I learned of Miss Havisham's death. Of Biddy, who was now a schoolteacher and who had taught Joe to read and write. Joe did everything for me, and I felt as if my whole life since I had left the forge was nothing but a fevered nightmare.

The day came that I was well enough for a carriage ride. Joe wrapped me up and carried me to the carriage as if I was still the small, helpless orphan to whom he had given a home.

But as I became stronger and better, Joe became less easy with me. In my state of weakness and dependence, he had called me the old names: "old Pip, old chap". But now he began to call me "sir".

It was my fault, I knew. All mine. I had given Joe so many reasons to doubt me. In becoming a gentleman, I had grown cold to him. How was I to convince him that I would not make that same mistake again?

We had talked so freely of the old days but never of the future. I had not told Joe I was in debt, partly because I was ashamed. But I also knew that he would want to help me, and this was a mess of my own making. I alone should make it right. I was forming a plan. Soon, soon, I would tell Joe what I intended to do.

We passed a most delightful Sunday, riding out to the country and walking in the fields. I decided I would confess my past mistakes on Monday. Then I would tell Joe what I planned for the future.

When I rose that Monday morning, I found a letter on the breakfast table:

I have departed, for you are well again, dear Pip, and will do better without me.

P.S. Ever the best of friends.

Enclosed in the letter was a note relating to the debt for which I had been arrested. Joe had paid the debt in full, and his name was on the receipt.

41

After three more days of rest and recovery, I followed Joe and returned to my childhood home. I thought it was for good. The June weather was delicious. The sky was blue, and the larks were soaring over the green corn. This was the day I would set things right, I'd decided.

I would go to the forge and apologise most humbly to Joe. And then I would go to Biddy. I would show her I was repentant. That I was humble. She had been fond of me once; she might be again. I would ask Biddy to marry me. And afterwards I would let her and Joe decide if I should return to the forge to work alongside him or if I should take on some other form of labour. All would be well.

I walked towards home listening for the clink of Joe's hammer. But all was still and quiet. I could hear nothing but the wind rustling the leaves. For the forge was closed.

But the house was not deserted. Inside were Biddy and Joe, standing close together, both neatly dressed.

I wept to see Biddy because she looked so pleasant and pretty. She wept to see me because I looked so worn and pale.

Crying, she said, "It's my wedding day, Pip! I am married to Joe."

My first thought was relief that I had not mentioned my plan to Joe. My second was that they would be the two happiest people I had ever known. I was truly delighted for them.

"Biddy, you have the best husband in the whole world," I said. "Dear, good, noble Joe, you have the best wife. You will be as happy as you deserve to be!"

I told them then that I was going away. I had a place as clerk to the company where Herbert was now a partner. I promised I would repay every farthing Joe had given to keep me out of prison. And there was one thing more I wished to say: "I hope you have children. And if you have a boy that reminds you of me – don't tell him I was thankless. Don't tell him I was ungenerous and unjust. Tell him that I honoured you both because you were both so good and true. Your child will surely grow up a much better man than I did."

42

I sold all I had. I went to Cairo and joined Herbert. I lived happily and plainly, and I paid back my debts.

I did not return to England and my childhood home for eleven years. But one December I found myself back there with Joe and Biddy and their children. A little girl, and a little boy, whom they had named Pip, for he did indeed remind them of me.

One evening, I sat up late talking with Biddy about the past.

I had heard that Estella had led a most unhappy life. Her husband had treated her with great cruelty. I had also heard that her husband had died from an accident caused by his ill treatment of a horse. But I had no idea what Estella was doing now or where she was. For all I knew, she had married again.

"Tell me, old friend," Biddy asked, "have you quite forgotten Estella?"

"I have forgotten nothing," I replied. "But that poor dream has gone, Biddy. I will never return there."

Even as I said it, I knew I lied. I planned to visit Satis House one last time before I returned to Cairo.

*

I walked to Satis House, but it was gone. Nothing was left but the ruined garden.

A cold, silvery mist was rising. The moon was not yet up, but the stars were shining and the evening was not yet dark. I could see where everything had once been. I was reconstructing it all in my mind when I saw a lone figure.

I walked towards it. As I drew nearer, it uttered my name and I cried out, "Estella!"

"I am greatly changed," she said. "I am surprised you recognise me."

The freshness of her beauty was indeed gone, but its incredible majesty and charm remained.

And there was something I had never seen before – a saddened, softened light in her once proud eyes.

And there was something I had never felt before – the friendly touch of Estella's once unfeeling hand.

"How strange we should meet here," I said, "where our first meeting was. Do you often come back?"

"I have never been here since," Estella replied.

"Nor I."

The moon began to rise. A silence came between us that Estella was the first to break.

"I have often hoped to return. Poor, poor old place!" she said, tears dropping from her eyes. "Were you wondering how it came to be in this condition? The ground still belongs to me, but that is the only thing that remains, the only thing not taken from me in all those wretched years."

"Is the ground to be built on?" I asked.

"Yes. I came to say goodbye to it," she said.

Another silence, which once again was broken by Estella.

"And you, Pip? You live abroad still?"

"Yes."

"I have often thought of you. Of late, very, very often. There was a long, hard time when I could not bear to think of what I had so carelessly thrown away when I did not know its worth. But now it has a place in my heart."

"You have always held your place in my heart, Estella," I said.

We were silent again until she said, "I had not thought to part with you here. But I am glad to do so."

"Glad to part again?" I asked. "To me it is a painful thing."

"But – do you remember? At our last parting, you said, 'God bless you; God forgive you!' If you could say that to me then, can you not say it now? Suffering has taught me to understand what your heart used to be. I have been bent and broken, but I hope into a better shape. Be as good to me now as you were then. Tell me we are friends."

"We are friends."

"And will continue friends apart," said Estella.

I took her hand in mine, and we went out of the ruined place. Just as the morning mists had risen when I'd first left the forge long ago, the evening mists were rising now. In all that expanse of calm light, I saw no shadow of another parting from Estella.

Our books are tested
for children and young people by
children and young people.

Thanks to everyone who consulted on
a manuscript for their time and effort in
helping us to make our books better
for our readers.